Mystery Adventure at
Longcliff Inn

By
Henry Bamman
Leonard Kennedy
Robert Whitehead

Illustrations
Roger Herrington

BENEFIC PRESS
Westchester, Illinois

MYSTERY ADVENTURE SERIES

Mystery Adventure of the Talking Statues
Mystery Adventure of the Jeweled Bell
Mystery Adventure at Cave Four

Mystery Adventure of the Indian Burial Ground
Mystery Adventure at Longcliff Inn
Mystery Adventure of the Smuggled Treasures

Edited by
Donna Juda

Library of Congress
Number 69-19640

Contents

Night in the Inn

"I'm glad you young people are here tonight," said Mrs. James. She turned in her chair and looked at the fireplace. There was a funny look on her face. "With Mr. James gone for the night, I don't like to stay here alone."

"What is it, Mrs. James? What are you afraid of?" asked Thad. He, Jeanine, and Bev were sitting on the floor in front of the fireplace.

"Oh, I'm really not afraid," laughed Mrs. James. "It's just that this old Inn is so big and dark when I'm here all alone."

Longcliff Inn was a rather frightening place. It was a big house, a house that had stood for over one hundred years. Just that day, when Thad, Jeanine, and Bev had come to the Inn, they had stopped on the road that led up from the harbor. They had looked for a long time at the old Inn. They had not been there for many months. Each time they came back, the old Inn seemed to be darker and bigger. All around it rose the big trees that were as old as the Inn itself. From the road, the youngsters could see only the roof and the chimneys. Here and there the sunlight hit a window and glinted through the trees.

The three friends had walked slowly toward the Inn, remembering all of the good times they had spent there. Mr. and Mrs. James had always made them welcome. There had been games in the big attic above the second floor, long, exciting slides down the rail of the staircase, and hours of climbing the trees in the garden.

There were many, many rooms in the old Inn. Some of them were big and light. From their windows one could look out at the harbor and the ocean beyond. But some of the rooms were small and dark, closed in by the big trees outside. As many times as the young people had been there, they had not been in all of the rooms of the old Inn.

Many years ago, Longcliff Inn had been a popular place filled with laughing, happy people. There had slept the sailors who roamed the seas and who stopped in Longcliff only to wait for another ship to take them away on new adventures. In the big living room of the Inn, traders had talked with the owners of ships and had bought their precious wares. Men and women from cities around the world had slept in the rooms of the Inn, walked in the lovely gardens, and gathered at the table for the fine food.

But that was when Longcliff was a bustling, exciting lumber and shipping town. Now the little town sat sleepily by the harbor, remembering those days of years ago. Only small fishing boats came in and out of the harbor. The new highway had gone around Longcliff, and today people drove by without knowing that an empty old Inn stood above the harbor, wishing for people to fill its rooms again, to laugh and sing and talk away the long nights.

Mrs. James arose from her chair and smiled at the young people. "I think it's about time you thought of going to bed," she said. "Where would you like to sleep tonight? You have a choice of a lot of rooms, you know."

Thad was sitting on the floor, his back against the fireplace. His face was thoughtful. He looked at Jeanine and Bev, who were lying on the bear rug that was spread in front of the fire.

"I—we would like to sleep right here, Mrs. James," said Thad. "We, uh, we brought our sleeping bags, and we'd like to sleep right here in front of the fire."

"That's nonsense!" said Mrs. James. "Here we have twenty good beds in the house, and you want to sleep on the floor. What are you thinking of?"

Jeanine looked carefully at her friends before she answered. "Well, Mrs. James, you know you've told us about the ghost that walks in the Inn at night. We thought we'd like to stay here tonight and see if we can hear him."

For just a moment, Mrs. James looked worried. Then she laughed. "Now, look here," she said. "We didn't want to frighten you. Those stories about the ghost are nonsense. You've been listening to Benjy again. I do wish Benjy wouldn't talk so much."

"But, Mrs. James," said Bev, "you and Mr. James both told us you thought there was a ghost here in the Inn. And, a while ago you said you didn't like to stay here alone."

"Well, we have heard strange noises lately," said Mrs. James. "But I think the idea of a ghost is simply foolish. This old Inn is so big and so old, and when I'm here alone, I hear every noise. Now, if you want to sleep on the floor, go ahead. I'm going to sleep in my nice, soft bed." With a wave of her hand, Mrs. James left the big living room and went down the hall to her room.

The youngsters rolled out their sleeping bags and were soon ready to turn in. Bev and Jeanine spread their bags in front of the fire. Thad was near the wall.

"Everyone ready?" asked Thad. Bev and Jeanine grunted sleepily. Thad reached out and turned off the light. The big room was plunged into deep shadows. Long fingers of light from the fire flickered across the floor and up the walls. Thad lay very still, listening to the quiet breathing of the two girls. He closed his eyes and started to drift into sleep.

"Cre-e-e-eak!" The noise cut through the room and the shadows seemed to leap up the walls.

Thad sat up. He looked quickly at the girls. They were sleeping peacefully, the light from the fire playing on their faces. Thad grinned and lay down again. "Silly of me," he murmured sleepily.

"Thump! Thump! Thump!" The noise was coming through the wall right by Thad's head. Now he sat up. He was wide awake. He felt a chill and realized that his hands were cold. There it was again! It seemed to be moving upward along the wall, scratching and thumping as it moved. Thad moved away from the wall. As he did, he noticed that Jeanine was sitting up. She had a horrified look on her face.

"Sh-h-h!" whispered Thad. He put his fingers to his lips and moved over to where Jeanine was sitting. "Don't make a sound!" Jeanine was staring at the wall, her eyes round and frightened.

"Oh, Thad, what is it?" she whispered. "Something's moving in that wall!" She crawled out of her sleeping bag and stood beside Thad. They stared at the wall.

There it was again! Slowly, slowly, something was moving on the other side of the wall.

"It sounds as if someone is walking up steps," whispered Thad, "but there isn't a stairway there!"

Bev was beginning to stir. Thad reached down and touched her on the shoulder, and she sat up and looked around wildly.

"What is it?" Bev screamed.

Both Thad and Jeanine moved beside Bev. Jeanine put her arm around Bev.

"It's nothing, Bev," Jeanine whispered. "We heard a strange sound. Don't make any more noise, please."

Thad stood up straight and tried very hard to look brave. "It's probably a rat in the wall," he said. But he didn't look as if he believed what he had said.

Jeanine and Bev didn't believe him either. They were huddled together on the rug, the light from the fire casting shadows on their faces. No one moved, but their eyes swept around the dark room and back to the wall by the fireplace. The old Inn was so quiet that only the sound of the branches of the trees moving softly against the windows could be heard.

"There it is again!" Thad's voice rang through the Inn.

The girls moved closer to Thad. Overhead they could hear the slow movement of footsteps. A board creaked and the sound rang through the Inn like a shot. The eyes of the three youngsters were glued to the ceiling above. Someone was walking around up there.

"It's right above us!" whispered Bev. "Someone's in the room right above us!"

"No, it can't be in the room above us," said Thad quietly. "It's above that. It's in the attic!"

There was a loud crash and it sounded as if someone had fallen over something.

"Mrs. James! Mrs. James!" Jeanine was screaming at the top of her lungs.

But Mrs. James was already in the room. She moved quickly over to the girls and put her arms around them.

"I heard it, too," she said quietly. "There must be something up there. I've heard it every night for over a week. Oh, I wish Mr. James were here!" She turned on the light, and the youngsters could see that she was worried.

"Probably rats," said Thad bravely. He looked from face to face. They didn't believe him, so he tried again. "Or maybe it's a raccoon. There are a lot of raccoons around here. Could they get into the attic, Mrs. James?"

Mrs. James laughed. "Of course, Thad! There's a broken window up there in the attic. That must be what it is." She smiled at the young people. "How about some hot chocolate now?" she asked.

"That sounds like a great idea," said Thad. "I'll help you, Mrs. James."

Thad and Mrs. James started toward the door to the kitchen. Just as Thad reached for the knob to the door, he turned and looked at Jeanine and Bev. The girls had sat down again on the rug before the fire.

"E-e-e-e-yow! Huh! Huh! Huh!" It sounded like the laugh of a madman or the cry of a wild animal. It rang through all the rooms of the old Inn and echoed away into silence. All four of the people in the room looked as if they were frozen. Then something fell down the big chimney. It hit the fire and sparks flew into the room.

(1600)

A Door in the Wall

"What a night!" said Thad as he stretched and got up. Jeanine and Bev were already up, and he could hear them moving in the kitchen. Thad looked thoughtfully at the wall, at the fireplace, and up at the ceiling of the big room. "That was no raccoon," he muttered to himself. "No raccoon ever laughed like that." He shook his head slowly as he walked into the kitchen.

Bev and Jeanine were eating breakfast. As Thad came through the door, they looked up with frightened faces.

"Oh, it's you!" breathed Jeanine.

"I thought you'd never wake up!" cried Bev.

"What's the matter with you two?" asked Thad. "You didn't let a little thing like a raccoon upset you, did you?" He tried hard to smile at them.

"Come off it, Thad," said Jeanine. "You didn't sleep any better than we did. Every time I woke up, you were stirring, too."

"There's no point in pretending that was a raccoon up there last night," remarked Bev. "There's something going on here in this house, and whatever it is, it isn't a raccoon. We know that!"

"Okay! Okay!" said Thad. He sat down and started eating his toast. "So maybe you're right, girls. I don't think it was a raccoon, either. And I intend to find out what it was!"

"Thad, we promised Mrs. James we wouldn't poke around," said Bev quickly. "She's gone to the store, and she made us promise that we wouldn't let you look around this house. Please, Thad, let's just go out into the garden and try to forget about last night."

"Forget about it?" cried Thad. "Are you girls out of your minds? You heard what I did last night. That laugh wasn't funny. Someone or something is not playing jokes. Whatever it is, it means business."

Then Thad stopped talking. Both of the girls were almost in tears.

"I'm sorry," said Thad. "Come on. Put your dishes away, and let's go outside. I want to look around the garden." He started out the side door of the kitchen.

"No you don't," cried Jeanine. She was right behind Thad. "You're not going to leave us in this house alone. Come on, Bev. Leave those dishes and let's get out of here."

Bev didn't need any urging. She and Jeanine followed Thad down the flight of steps and out under the big trees in the garden. The sun was shining, and long fingers of light poked through the branches of the trees and touched the grass below. Thad stood for a long time looking at the wall of the house. Both of the girls watched him, wondering what he was thinking about. Suddenly, there was a loud snapping noise, and Thad and the two girls whirled around.

"Getting some fresh air?" The speaker was an old man.

"Hello, Benjy!" said Thad. "We haven't seen you for a long time. How have you been?"

Benjy looked all around him, but he didn't look at the youngsters. He chuckled to himself. "I'm all right!" he said. "How about you? Are you here to stay?"

Benjy was the gardener who had been with Mr. and Mrs. James for many years. Thad and the girls could never remember a time when Benjy had been friendly. During all the times they had been at the Inn, none of the youngsters could remember seeing Benjy smile. He went about his work slowly, keeping to himself.

"We....uh....we are just looking around, Benjy," said Thad. "Yes, we came to stay for a few days. Is everything here all right?"

Benjy started to walk away, shaking his head. "Nothing's all right," he muttered. "You'll see! You'll see! You'd better go home, all of you." He stepped behind a big tree and disappeared among the bushes.

"I don't like him," said Bev. "What do you think he meant by that?"

Thad laughed. "Now, don't let Benjy upset you, girls," he answered. "You know how he is. Benjy doesn't mean anything by what he says. I think he just doesn't like having anyone else around." He started to walk back toward the house.

Thad led the way up the steps into the kitchen. He sat down at the table and had a glass of milk. He said nothing. The girls started washing and drying their dishes. Quietly, Thad moved out of his chair and walked softly toward the door leading into the living room. At the door he looked back. Jeanine and Bev were chattering away. They hadn't seen him leave.

Quickly, Thad moved over near the wall where he had
slept the night before. For a long time he let his eyes move
over the panels of the boards above the place where he had
slept. Then he put his hands on the panels and felt each
crack. Slowly, slowly, his hands moved over the boards.
Now one hand slid up and down a board. He gave the
board a push, and it moved! He pushed harder, and a
part of the wall was swinging into the room.

For a moment, Thad caught his breath. "Wow! What
have we here?" he whispered. He pushed harder on the
board, and the wall moved still further. Slowly, a hole
was opening.

"Thad!" screamed a voice. "What are you doing?"

Thad whirled around. Bev was standing there, her
hands over her mouth, her eyes big as saucers.

"Bev! Don't ever shout at me like that!" cried Thad. "You nearly scared the wits out of me!" He moved back from the wall. Just as he did, Jeanine came into the room.

All three of them stood for a minute looking at the hole in the wall. It was certainly a door.

"I've really found something," whispered Thad. "Now I think I know where our friend was last night." He shivered as he looked into the darkness of the doorway.

"Please, Thad, let's leave it alone until Mrs. James comes back," cried Jeanine.

Thad seemed to be talking to himself. "I knew there was something in that wall," he muttered. "When I was standing outside, I could tell that the wall on this side of the house was very thick—much too thick for a plain wall. There's something behind that door, and I'm going to find out what it is."

"I'm going with you!" cried Bev. "You can stay here if you want to, Jeanine. I'm going to help Thad."

"Who said I wanted to stay here?" asked Jeanine. "Just try to leave me behind. But are you going to crawl through that door? Why don't we wait until Mrs. James comes home? Or, let's go get Benjy."

"Benjy!" snorted Thad. "Now how do you think Benjy could help us? He's afraid of his own shadow."

Jeanine had walked over and given the board another push. Now the door in the wall was wide open. It looked just big enough for someone to crawl through it.

"Someone get a flashlight," said Jeanine. "I want to see what's in there."

Thad got a flashlight which was near the fireplace and the three of them looked into the hole in the wall. As the light moved through the darkness, they could see a wall

beyond. Thad moved the flashlight upward, and then he
gasped loudly.

"There are steps in there!"
he whispered. "Come on, let's
find out where they go!" He
started to crawl through the
hole. Slowly he felt around
him, and he was standing on
the steps. Then he poked his
head back into the room.
"Come on, you two," he said.
"I'm not going up there alone."

Jeanine crawled through the
hole and then Bev came. In
the light from the flashlight,
their faces looked pale.

"It smells so musty in here,"
whispered Bev. She was holding Jeanine's arm.

"It feels awful. I wish we'd
go back," said Jeanine.

Thad turned the light into
the girls' faces. "Now listen!
We're going to go up those
stairs and find out where
they go," he said. His voice
rang so loudly that he lowered
it almost to a whisper. He
could hear the echo of his voice
as it bounced through the
darkness above.

"Go ahead, Thad," said Jeanine calmly. "We're going with you. Let me hold the flashlight. You go ahead. Bev, you follow me."

One by one they climbed the steps. Jeanine swung the light up and down. On all sides there was nothing but darkness. Cobwebs brushed against their faces.

"Boy, these steps really go up," whispered Thad. "Watch out! There's a turn here." In the light, the girls saw him as he went around a corner.

Just then, something came down the steps—something big and moving rapidly. It brushed by Thad and turned the corner. For a moment, Jeanine stared. Then she screamed.

"The flashlight! Someone took the flashlight!" Jeanine cried. She was clinging to Bev. Thad moved closer to them. They stood there in the darkness, hardly daring to breathe. As they listened, they heard the sound of footsteps going down, down the steps. They didn't move until the footsteps had died away.

"Easy," whispered Thad. "Let's get back down to the living room. Here, hold on to me. I'll lead you down." Slowly, he moved down the stairs, counting as he went. Suddenly, he stopped.

"It isn't here!" he cried. "The door! The door is closed. We've been locked in."

Out of the darkness a small bat swooped against Bev's head. Bev screamed, and Jeanine screamed, too.

From a distance came a horrible sound. "E-e-e-yow! Huh! Huh!"

(1601)

Rescued

"What's the matter up there?" a voice called from the bottom of the steps. A door opened and light streamed up the steps. Someone was standing in the open doorway.

"Mr. James!" shouted Thad. "We're up here. It's Thad, and Jeanine, and Bev."

"Well, come on down here," said Mr. James. "What on earth are you doing on those old steps?"

By now the youngsters had come down the steps and gone through the door. They looked around them and saw that they were in the basement of the Inn.

"Where did he go?" cried Jeanine. Her face was white, and there were cobwebs in her hair. "Did he get away?"

Mr. James shook his head. "Where did he go?" he laughed. "What are you talking about?"

All three of the young people started talking at once. Finally, Mr. James held up his hand and said, "Now, wait a minute. Let's get the story straight. Come on, let's go upstairs and you can tell me all about it." He led the way out of the basement, and they came out into the garden. Mr. James sat down on a bench and smiled at the youngsters. "Tell me about it," he said.

Slowly, Thad told Mr. James about their night in the Inn. As he talked, Thad watched Mr. James closely. Mr. James was smiling, but suddenly he was very thoughtful, and then he looked worried. Then he stopped Thad.

"Let me get this straight, Thad. You really heard someone laugh, did you?"

"Oh, yes, it was a horrible laugh!" cried Jeanine.

"It was the same laugh that we heard just a few minutes ago up there on the steps!" said Bev.

"I saw him! I really did!" cried Jeanine. "It was a man, an old man. He looked horrible. I had the flashlight turned right on him. Then he grabbed the flashlight."

"Did you see his face?" asked Mr. James.

"Yes, well....no, I really didn't," answered Jeanine. "I saw it, but I didn't. Oh, do you know what I mean?"

"You must have been very frightened, Jeanine," said Mr. James softly. "Try to remember, though. Was it an old man? You said it was."

Jeanine nodded. "Yes, he was old. He had white hair, and it was long. It was long like...." Suddenly, Jeanine clapped her hand over her mouth.

"Like what, Jeanine? What were you going to say?" Thad and Bev cried.

"Like Benjy's hair!" cried Jeanine. "Only I don't think it was Benjy. I saw a little of the man's face, and he didn't look like Benjy."

"It couldn't have been Benjy," said Mr. James. "Benjy was leaving for town just as I came home. I met him on the road. He seemed terribly upset about something, but Benjy is usually upset about something," He turned to Thad. "Go on with your story, Thad. How did you get to those steps?"

Thad and the girls told Mr. James about the door in the wall. Mr. James was very surprised. "A door in the wall?" he cried. "I certainly didn't know about that!"

Thad led the way into the house. All of them stood in the living room as Thad moved his hand over the boards. Slowly, the door in the wall opened. No one said a word.

"Well, I'll be!" said Mr. James. "I've lived here all my life, and I didn't know that door was there. Now that explains everything...."

"What? What does it explain?" cried Thad.

"Oh, nothing, Thad. Let's forget about it," said Mr. James. He turned away. Then he turned back to the three young people. They were standing there with their backs to the fireplace, looking frightened.

"No, I'm not going to do that to you," said Mr. James. "I'm going to tell you the truth. You found the door, and you've just had a terrible time on those steps. I'll tell you everything." With a sigh, he sat down in a big chair. He motioned the young people to sit down, too. They sat on the floor, looking up into his kind face.

"You see, something strange has been going on here for quite a while," said Mr. James slowly. "Oh, there's always been talk of a ghost in this old Inn, but Mrs. James and I have always laughed at that story. But lately we've heard strange noises at night, like someone moving around up in the attic. I've gone up there two or three times, and I found nothing. But, then, things started happening down here." He waved his hand around the living room. "I've heard noises in here at night. Someone was getting in, and for the life of me I couldn't find out how. All of the doors and windows were locked."

"The door in the wall!" said Bev. "He came through the door in the wall!"

"You're probably right, Bev," answered Mr. James. "That must be the answer. Several times Mrs. James found dirty footprints on the rug, and we knew someone had been here."

Jeanine had moved over until she was sitting against Mr. James. "What do you suppose he wants?" she whispered. "He must be looking for something, or he wouldn't keep coming back like that."

"I wish I knew the answer to that question, Jeanine," said Mr. James. "Then maybe we could sleep better. I'll tell you, I haven't slept much for a long time."

Thad had been pacing back and forth in the room. Then he stopped and looked intently at Mr. James.

"Mr. James, who knows about those steps in that wall? Does Benjy know about them? We've been here lots of times, and we've played in the basement, but we didn't know about that door that you opened."

Mr. James didn't answer for a moment. Then his words came out slowly and thoughtfully. "Yes, Benjy knows about the steps. Years ago we used those steps to take things up to the attic. You see, when the old Inn was full of people, as it was many years ago, we used the attic to store our supplies. And, sometimes we let people sleep up there, when our beds were full and there wasn't any other place to sleep. We had a few cots up there. In fact, I guess they're still there." Mr. James stopped and looked at Thad. "Why did you ask about Benjy, Thad?" he asked.

"I really don't know," replied Thad. "I'm just trying to fit the pieces together. Benjy said some strange things to us this morning when we were out in the garden. I thought he was warning us not to stay around here."

"The garden! That reminds me," cried Mr. James, jumping to his feet. "Come on, you three. I want to find out about something."

Mr. James went through the kitchen, down the steps, and out through the garden. He ducked under the trees and stopped beside a clump of bushes. He stood there, looking down at the ground. "That's strange," he said. "It has been moved."

Thad, Jeanine, and Bev were standing right beside Mr. James. They looked all around, but they could see nothing. Mr. James continued to stare at the spot on the ground. Then Thad saw some old boards that seemed to have been moved. The soil had been pushed away.

"What is it?" cried Jeanine. "What do you see? Mr. James, what are you looking at?"

"It was Old Sam," said Mr. James, slowly. "Just as we came out of the basement into the garden, I saw Old Sam. He seemed to come right up out of the ground, and then he went off through the bushes. I was so busy listening to you, I didn't think anything about it. Old Sam hangs around town a lot, but what was he doing in this garden?"

"What's under those boards, Mr. James?" asked Thad.

"That's an old well, Thad. It's been closed for years. In fact, I don't think we ever used it. What are you thinking of, Thad?"

"Just this," replied Thad. He dropped to his knees and lifted one of the boards. Then he lifted another. Mr. James helped him. One by one, the boards were lifted, and the four of them stood there looking down into the old well. It was nearly five feet across, and its walls were lined with bricks.

"Girls!" shouted Mr. James, "Go into the kitchen and get my big flashlight. Hurry!"

Jeanine and Bev ran as fast as they could. They were soon back by the well, excited and panting. Mr. James took the flashlight from Bev and knelt beside the well.

"Would you look at that!" he cried. Thad, Bev, and Jeanine crept to the edge of the well and looked down. On the far side of the wall of the well, they saw a big hole.

"I'm going down," said Thad. He started to climb over the edge of the well, but Mr. James pulled him back.

"Now don't get too excited, Thad," said Mr. James. "Let's get a rope to hold you with. We have no idea what's at the bottom of this well." He went to a small shed and returned with a rope. Carefully he tied it around Thad and looped the rope over the branch of a big tree that hung over the well. "Now, Thad! Down you go!"

Thad slowly moved down the wall of the well. Mr. James and the girls held on to the rope, letting it out inch by inch as Thad went down.

"Wow!" cried Thad from down in the well.

"What is it? What have you found?" cried Mr. James. He and the girls let go of the rope and looked down into the well. Thad was standing at the bottom, holding the flashlight toward the hole in the wall of the well.

"A tunnel!" shouted Thad. "A tunnel lined with bricks! And it goes back toward the house!" (1648)

The Tunnel

Mr. James brought a ladder. One by one, they went down into the well and looked at the tunnel. Mr. James and Thad walked a few feet into the tunnel, flashing their light before them. In the distance the tunnel turned upward, and they could see that there were steps.

"Let's get out of here," said Mr. James, suddenly. Within a few minutes, all of them were back in the garden. They continued to look at the well, each person wondering.

"This is going to call for some planning," said Mr. James. "Let's cover the well exactly as it was. Someone is using that well to get into the Inn. Why, I don't know, but I intend to find out." He looked at the faces of the three young people. "I may need you to help me," he said. "But first you must promise not to say anything.'

"Oh, we won't say a word," said Jeanine.

"You can count on me," said Bev. "I won't tell anyone."

"How about Mrs. James?" asked Thad. "Aren't we going to tell her?"

"I'll tell her," said Mr. James. "But, I don't want to frighten her more than I have to. We don't know what we're dealing with here. Someone wants something that's in the inn. He may be dangerous."

The well was covered. Soil and leaves were scattered over the boards again. Mr. James turned toward the house. Thad and the girls followed him. Suddenly, a cloud covered the sun, and the garden was in shadows. Jeanine shivered and moved closer to Bev.

Thad stopped once, and there was a strange look on his face. Then he quickly caught up with the others as they went into the kitchen.

Mrs. James was there, bustling about the kitchen. When she saw Mr. James' face, she looked at him carefully. "What's wrong?" she asked. "Has something happened?"

"Mother," said Mr. James quietly, "I think you'd better come into the living room. We need to talk to you."

After everyone was seated, Mr. James quickly told Mrs. James about what had happened. As Mrs. James listened, she nodded her head again and again.

"I knew it! I knew it!" she said. "We've tried to pretend that nothing was wrong, but I just knew that someone was in this house. And after that awful laugh last night, and the sounds in that wall, I just knew that we were in danger," she added emphatically.

"Maybe not in danger, Mother," said Mr. James softly. "Let's not think of it that way. Maybe someone is just snooping around seeing what he can find. He probably is not dangerous, or he would have caused more trouble than he has. Whoever it is, he's looking for something, and we have to figure out what he's looking for."

Suddenly, Bev sat up and looked directly at Mr. James. "Who is Old Sam?" she asked.

Mrs. James laughed. "Oh, he's a harmless old man. Old Sam has lived here for several months. I don't know where he came from. He lives in a little cabin back in the woods. He wouldn't harm anyone. He doesn't talk to anyone. He just roams around, and he comes to town when he needs to buy something."

"But what was he doing in your garden?" asked Jeanine. "Mr. James saw him there right after we met that man on the steps."

Mrs. James turned to her husband. "Old Sam? In our garden? When did you see him?"

Mr. James explained how he had seen Old Sam. "I guess I forgot to mention him," he said.

"Well, he must have been looking for Benjy," said Mrs. James. "Benjy is the only person Old Sam talks to. I see them together now and then when Old Sam comes to town."

"I didn't know that!" exclaimed Mr. James. "I didn't know that Benjy ever talked to anyone! Old Sam and Benjy! That's a pair for you!"

"Mr. James, didn't you tell me that Benjy wasn't here this morning?" asked Thad. Everyone turned and looked at Mr. James.

"He went off to town, just as I said," said Mr. James. "Why do you ask?"

"Because I saw him!" cried Thad. "When we were coming into the house a few minutes ago, Benjy was there, behind a bush. He was looking at us, and he had a mean look on his face."

"Oh, that's the way Benjy is," said Mr. James. "He probably didn't stay in town very long. Don't worry about Benjy. He may look mean, but he wouldn't harm a flea."

Mrs. James had moved out to the kitchen and had started to fix lunch. Mr. James followed her, and the youngsters could hear the old couple talking quietly.

Suddenly, Jeanine jumped to her feet. She put her fingers to her lips and moved over close to Thad and Bev. "Sh! Don't say anything," she said. "I want to talk to both of you. Let's go out into the garden."

Thad and Bev followed Jeanine.

"Now stay out of trouble," smiled Mr. James as the youngsters went out of the door.

Thad paused and looked back. "Don't worry," he replied. I think we've had about enough for one day."

Bev and Jeanine were sitting in the sun, talking like a couple of birds. As Thad came up to them, they looked all around. Then Jeanine motioned to Thad to sit down beside them. As he sat down, Thad looked around, too. There was no sign of Benjy.

"I've got a plan," said Jeanine in a low voice.

"Oh, no, you don't," groaned Thad. "We told Mr. James we'd stay out of this thing. Now don't go getting ideas, Jeanine. You know how we can get into trouble when you get a wild idea."

Jeanine paid no attention to Thad. "We'll have to go there ourselves," she said finally.

"Go where?" asked Bev. "Jeanine, what on earth are you talking about?"

"We're going to find out about Old Sam," said Jeanine. "I know that wasn't Benjy on those steps this morning. It must have been Old Sam. Thad, you know where Old Sam lives. It's that old cabin back in the woods about a mile from here. Someone said just a few days ago that an old man was living in the cabin now."

Thad stood up and looked sternly at Jeanine. "I don't know what you're thinking of," he said firmly. "But we are not going to mess around with this thing. Someone might get hurt."

Now it was Bev's turn. She turned to Thad, and she looked angry. "I don't know what's wrong with you, Thad," she said. "Are you afraid? If you are, Jeanine and I will just have to go alone."

Thad looked defeated. "But, what on earth do you expect to find?" he cried. "What good will it do to go snooping around Old Sam's cabin?"

"That's just it, Thad," answered Jeanine. "We don't know anything now except that someone is getting into the old Inn and Mr. and Mrs. James are frightened.

They're very old people, Thad, and they really need help. We'll be careful. We just need to find out what's going on, and Old Sam just might be able to give us the answer."

"Okay, have your way," shrugged Thad. "I can see there's no need of trying to keep you two from going. You can count on me. When do we go?"

"We'll go right after lunch," said Jeanine. "We know those woods as well as we know our own backyards. We'll just go over there and see what we can find out."

"Right," said Thad. "We can't get lost."

When Mrs. James called the youngsters to lunch, they got up and walked slowly toward the house.

"Now remember, you're not to say a word to anyone," said Bev. "We'll tell Mrs. James we're going for a walk, and we'll take off for the woods."

Both Thad and Jeanine nodded. For just a moment, they stopped and looked around them. There was no sight of Benjy as they went in to lunch. But, from among the bushes, a pair of eyes watched the three young people as they went up the steps and into the old Inn.

The Map

The road led down a hill through the thick trees, and then it seemed to go nowhere. Thad, Jeanine, and Bev walked slowly as if they were out for an afternoon's walk. Now and then they stopped to look at a tree, a flower, or a bird. Each time they paused, they looked around, too. Now the road ended, and they stood at the edge of the woods, looking through the thick trees.

"I think Mrs. James knows what we're doing," said Bev. "When I told her we were going for a walk, she said,

'If you follow the road to its end, you'll find a path that leads right into the woods.' She must have known."

"We're almost there," said Thad. "The cabin is just over that hill. We'll have to be careful now. No talking, understand? Let's all stick together. If you follow me, I think I can get to the cabin without being seen." He stepped off the path and headed through the brush.

Bev and Jeanine followed quietly behind him. Now and then he held a limb of a small tree until they had passed. There wasn't a sound in the woods, except the chatter of squirrels and the call of a lone bird. The big

trees were so thick above their heads that the sun came through only in a few places. Their feet sank into the soft, green moss that covered the ground.

They had almost reached the cabin when a blue jay screamed at them. Thad froze in his tracks, and Jeanine and Bev sat down on their heels. It was so quiet that they could hear each other breathing.

"Stay here," whispered Thad. "I'll go ahead and look the place over. Remember, don't move. I'll be back just as soon as I can."

He moved quickly but softly through the thick brush, and then he was gone.

Bev looked all around her. She didn't appear to be too brave. "I hope Thad doesn't get lost," she said. "If anything happens, let's run back to the road."

"Thad won't get lost," said Jeanine as she settled comfortably against a tree. "He knows these woods as well as anyone does. We'll just have to wait and be patient." She closed her eyes and rested. Not too far away there was a small stream, and the sound of running, gurgling water reached the girls. Bev curled up on the soft moss

beside Jeanine and closed her eyes. Each of the girls was thinking. The night before had been a frightening one, and they had not slept well. The quiet twitter of birds and the murmuring of the little stream were too much for the tired girls. Within a short time, both were sleeping.

"Bev! Jeanine! Wake up. Come on, we have to go!" It was Thad, and there was a look on his face that told the girls that he was excited.

"What .... what's wrong?" asked Bev, rubbing her eyes.

"Bev, Bev, get up! I've been to the cabin. Come on, now, both of you." Thad started off through the woods.

Jeanine and Bev followed him, stepping softly and working their way through the brush. Then Thad stopped and held up his hand. He squatted down and pointed. The girls knelt beside him and peered through the brush.

The cabin was very small, not more than one room, and it looked very old and lonely. Brush grew up all around it. From the chimney came a thin wisp of blue smoke, and a ray of sunlight glinted on the only window.

"We'll stay right here," whispered Thad. "This is a good hiding place."

"Did you see Old Sam?" asked Jeanine.

"He's in the cabin," answered Thad. "I saw him carry some wood in for the fire just before I came back to you. We'll just have to wait here and watch for him."

All three of the youngsters settled down on the soft ground. Nearby a squirrel chattered at them and then scurried off through the tree tops. The three pair of eyes remained on the little cabin. For a long time no sound was heard, and no one moved. Then the door of the cabin opened, and someone was coming out.

An old man stepped out of the door of the cabin. He
stood on the doorstep and looked around him. Then he
picked up an axe and started toward where the youngsters
were hiding.

"Let's get out of here," whispered Bev.

"Hold it, Bev!" said Thad. "Don't move! He can't
know we're here."

The old man came slowly toward them, but then he
stopped. He saw a dead tree and started swinging the
axe, cutting wood.

"Is that the man you saw this morning, Jeanine?" whispered Thad.

They could see the old man's face clearly. It wasn't a mean face at all. As he swung the axe again and again, the old man started whistling.

"He had hair like that," whispered Jeanine. "But I don't think that's the same man. That was a big man on the steps. And his face looked ugly."

"Well, if that's Old Sam, he isn't a very big man," said Bev. "I think he has a nice face."

Old Sam had finished chopping wood. He laid his axe down and gathered an armful of wood. Slowly he walked toward the cabin and went inside.

Just then a group of blue jays started screaming. They flew down and swooped low over the three youngsters. "Jay! Jay!" they cried. Lower and lower they came, screaming loudly.

The door of the cabin opened again, and Old Sam stepped out. In his hands he held a long gun. He stood on the doorstep, looking around. He seemed to look right at the youngsters. He walked slowly toward them, watching the jay birds. When he was not more than twenty feet away, the jay birds gave one last scream and flew away into the tops of the tall trees. Old Sam stood for a minute, peering at the bushes. Then he shrugged and turned back to the cabin and went in.

"Whew!" said Bev. "That was a close one! We'd better get out of here before those jays come back again."

"I agree," said Thad. "Let's go back to the stream and wait for darkness. We can't find out anything as long as there is light." He bent down low and started away. The two girls followed him. When they reached a thick clump of bushes, they stopped and sat down.

"Now what?" asked Jeanine. "If we don't get back before dark, Mr. and Mrs. James will start looking for us. If Mrs. James knew that we were coming, this is the first place they'll look."

"We're going to wait," said Thad firmly. "This was your idea, Jeanine, and we're going to stick it out. When it gets dark, we can get up close to that cabin and watch Old Sam. We're not going back until we find out what he's up to."

It seemed to Bev that darkness would never come. But when the sun dropped behind the trees, the shadows stole softly but quickly through the woods. Within a few minutes everything was dark.

"Let's go!" said Thad. "Now here's the plan. You two stand watch, and I'm going to go up and look through the window into that cabin. If you hear anything or see anything, you whistle, and we'll take off on a run."

Just as they came near the cabin, Thad stopped again. All three of them stood still and looked around. Through the window of the cabin they could see a light. Old Sam was nowhere to be seen.

"Stay right here," said Thad. "Remember to watch and to whistle if you see anything."

"You're not going, Thad. I am," said Jeanine. "This was my idea. You stay here with Bev. I'm smaller than

you and I can get up to that window easier than you can."
Jeanine stepped out from the bushes and before they could
stop her, she had disappeared in the darkness.

Thad and Bev stood with their eyes glued on the window of the little cabin. Light streamed from the window
and on the bushes outside. As they watched, hardly breathing, they saw Jeanine's head against the light. She was
looking through the window!

"Oh, why doesn't she stay down!" cried Bev. "Old
Sam will see her!"

For a long time Jeanine stood there peering through the
window. Then her head disappeared in the darkness, and
suddenly she was there beside them. She motioned for them
to follow her, and the three of them moved quickly
through the brush and trees. When they reached the stream,
Jeanine stopped them.

"Oh, Thad! Bev! You'll never believe it!" she said.
"What did you see? Tell us!" cried Bev.

Jeanine gasped for breath and gulped before she spoke. In the dim light her eyes were shining with excitement.

"He has a map," she said. "Old Sam has a map. He was sitting at a table, right by that window, and I could see everything he was doing. He was reading a letter and looking at a map."

"What's so great about a map?" asked Thad. "What was the map? Do you know?"

"I sure do," cried Jeanine. "It was a map of Longcliff Inn showing all of the rooms. And it showed that tunnel to the well, too!"

(1485)

The Trap

"And you really saw Old Sam with a map of Longcliff Inn, Jeanine?" asked Mr. James.

The youngsters were sitting in the living room of the old inn talking with Mr. and Mrs. James. They had come in only a short time before. At first, Mr. James had been angry with them for going off alone to Old Sam's cabin, but as he had listened to their story, he had begun to smile.

"It really was a map of the inn, Mr. James," said Jeanine. "I wasn't more than three feet away from Old Sam, and I could see the map very well."

"Well, now we have something to go on," said Mr. James. "We know, or we think we know, that Old Sam has something to do with the inn. And, since I saw him come out of the well this morning, he must be the person who has been walking around here at night. But what on earth would Old Sam be looking for, and where did he get that map of this inn?" Mr. James looked very puzzled. "This has me stumped," he added.

"Jeanine said that the map looked very old," said Thad. "At some time or other someone went to the trouble to make that map. And that someone must have left something in the inn that Old Sam is looking for."

Mr. James nodded. "Yes, that's very possible. Hundreds of people have stayed in this Inn since it was built —all kinds of people. Rich men, poor men, sailors, bankers—they all came to the Inn at one time. And one of those persons could have hidden something in the Inn that he planned to come back for later. But, where does Old Sam fit into this puzzle?"

"It seems to me that there is only one way to find out," said Bev. "Old Sam doesn't know that we saw him with that map. He doesn't know that you saw him in the garden. I'll bet he'll be back—maybe tonight."

Thad jumped to his feet. "I think you're right, Bev. We need to set a trap, Mr. James. Isn't there some way that we could wait and catch Old Sam if he comes back to the Inn?"

For a moment Mr. James looked thoughtful. "I think I know the kind of trap that we can set," he said finally. "Let's wait until he enters the well. Then, when we think that he has had time to reach the house, we'll fix the cover of that well so he can't get back out of it. I'll go up to the attic through the door in the basement. You can go to the attic through the only other door that leads from the second floor. If we catch Old Sam in the attic, he'll have to tell us what it is he's up to."

They laid their plans carefully after that. They checked each plan until everyone knew exactly what was to be done. Finally, Mr. James turned to Mrs. James and said, "Mother, you go to bed now, just as you always do. Whatever happens, you stay out of the way. We wouldn't want you to get hurt. But when you hear us come into the house, maybe you'd better watch that door in the wall. If anyone comes out of it, yell for all you're worth."

"I'll do more than that!" said Mrs. James. She walked over to the fireplace and picked up a big piece of wood. "If anyone comes through that wall, he'll wish he hadn't." She looked so serious as she stood there with the piece of wood, that all of them laughed.

"We'd better hurry," said Jeanine. "It's ten o'clock now, and if Old Sam is coming tonight, he should be here soon. Come on, let's get into the garden."

They had planned to wait in the garden near the old well to be sure that Old Sam came. Then, when he was in the well and the well had been closed off, they would go to the Inn and trap him. Mr. James and the three youngsters moved through the dark kitchen to the door. Quietly they went down the steps and into the garden. When they were halfway through the garden, Mr. James whispered, "Here, take my hand. Each person hold on to another person. I know the way here, and I'll keep you from bumping into anything." Slowly he led them in the darkness to a clump of bushes that stood about ten feet from the old well. Then they all waited.

The night was almost too quiet. There wasn't a sound in the air. The four of them huddled together waiting, waiting. Almost as if someone had turned it on, the moon came over the roof of the old Inn and flooded the garden with white light. Bev, Thad, and Jeanine sat without moving. Their eyes turned this way and that, but all they could see were deep shadows.

Then they heard noises like shuffling footsteps. Someone was walking toward them. They could see a dim figure moving in the shadows. Closer and closer the figure came. The person was coming right toward them!

Thad could tell that it was the figure of an old man, but he couldn't see the face. Now the man came right up to the clump of bushes and almost touched Thad. At that moment, Thad decided to act.

"Grab him!" shouted Thad, and he jumped at the old man. He grabbed the man by the legs, and the old man fell to the ground.

"Let me go! Let me go!" cried the voice of the old man, but Thad, Jeanine, and Bev were all sitting on top of him.

Just then the light from the moon hit the old man in the face.

"Benjy!" cried Mr. James. "So it was you all the time!"

Thad, and the two girls stood up. Benjy, more frightened than he had ever been before, lay on the ground and looked at Mr. James and the youngsters.

"Please, Mr. James, don't let them go. I know I shouldn't be keeping them here in the garden, but they're such nice pets," cried Benjy.

"What are you talking about? Let what go?" asked Mr. James. "Benjy, get up off that ground and explain what you're doing down here. What are you doing here by this well?"

Benjy stood up. He still looked very frightened. He looked at the faces of the young people and then at Mr. James. "I wasn't doing anything by the well, Mr. James," he answered. "I don't know anything about a well. I was just coming down here to feed my babies."

"Feed your what?" asked Thad. "Did you say babies?"

Benjy hung his head. "That's what I call them," he said softly. "They're my pets. Mr. James never wanted them around, and I shouldn't have kept them."

"Benjy, will you tell me what you are talking about?" said Mr. James.

"The raccoons, Mr. James. I've got a pen of raccoons back there behind those bushes. You never come down to this part of the garden, and I have so enjoyed keeping them," Benjy sighed. "I know that raccoons eat your sweet corn and get into the attic of the house, but I did so want to keep them for pets. They were so little when I found them, and I....well, I just kept them."

Mr. James chuckled. "Well, I'll be!" he said. "Now listen, Benjy, and tell me the truth. Don't you know about that old well? Have you been going down in the well? Have you been up in the attic of the Inn at night?"

Benjy looked confused. "Mr. James, I told you I don't know anything about a well. And what are you saying about my being in the attic at night? You know I wouldn't do anything like that."

"It's all right, Benjy," said Mr. James. "But you must tell me something. Do you know Old Sam, the fellow who lives in the cabin in the woods? Is he a friend of yours, Benjy?"

Benjy hesitated for a moment. "Yes, sir, I know him," he answered. "He's always trying to talk to me. He's an odd old fellow. I really don't like him."

"What does Old Sam talk to you about, Benjy?" asked Jeanine. "Does he ask you questions?"

"Why, yes, miss. He does ask me questions," replied Benjy. "He's always asking about....well, he asks questions about the old Inn." He turned to Mr. James. "I've never told him anything about the Inn, Mr. James. He's asked a lot of questions, but I can't figure out why he wants to know so much."

"Benjy, we may need your help before the night is over," said Mr. James. Quickly he told Benjy about the well, the tunnel, and the man in the attic of the old Inn. Benjy listened carefully. Then he looked as if he might cry.

"Oh, Mr. James, and you thought I was the one who was snooping around in your house!" he cried.

Mr. James patted Benjy on the back and smiled at the old man. "Benjy, please try to understand. We have been very frightened. Someone has been breaking into the

Inn for a long time now. Mrs. James and I have not known what to do about it. We're out here right now, trying to trap whoever it is who's been getting into the Inn. Will you help us?"

"I'll do anything you say, Mr. James," said Benjy.

"We can use you, Benjy," said Bev. "You come with us when we have to go up those steps to the attic."

"Sh-h-h!" cried Jeanine. "Everyone sit down! Get out of sight! I just saw someone down there." She pointed to the lower end of the garden.

Everyone stooped down in the bushes. All eyes watched the corner of the garden. Then, the figure of an old man stepped into the moonlight.

Jeanine gasped. "That's Old Sam!" she whispered.

Old Sam came straight to the well. He didn't look left or right. When he reached the well, he leaned over and moved one of the boards aside. Slowly, he crawled through the opening and disappeared.

"Don't move yet," whispered Mr. James. "Give him time to get to the Inn."

They could have heard a pin drop it was so quiet in the garden. But from down in the well they heard footsteps that slowly moved farther away.

"Now!" cried Mr. James. "Move fast!"

Jeanine, Thad, and Bev grabbed the heavy pieces of wood that they had hidden in the bushes. With the help of Mr. James and Benjy, they put the wood over the well. Then Mr. James rolled two big rocks on the boards.

"Just to be sure," he said. "Now our trap is half set! Let's get into the Inn now. I'll see you in the attic in about five minutes! I think we're about to catch him!"

All five of them ran toward the Inn.

(1851)

Into the Attic

When they reached the living room, Thad, Jeanine, and Bev found Mrs. James sitting by the fireplace. In her hands Mrs. James held a big piece of wood. The youngsters almost laughed when they saw her face.

"He's up there!" said Mrs. James. "I heard him go up the steps into the attic. He'd better not come down here!" Then she noticed that Benjy was standing in the room, too. "Benjy! What on earth are you doing here at this hour of the night?"

"We'll explain later, Mrs. James," said Thad. "Right now, we'd better get up those steps." He looked at the girls and at Benjy. "Move quietly, now. Try not to make any noise on the steps."

Slowly the four of them moved up the steps to the second floor. There was no light in the rooms, and shadows lay everywhere. Jeanine and Bev stayed very close to each other. In the empty rooms their footsteps sounded loud and rang through the old Inn. Suddenly, Thad stopped. Standing in the moonlight in front of a door, he whispered, "This leads up to the attic. Now remember not to make any noise if you can help it. If we see Old Sam, let's watch him. If we jump him, we may never find out what he is looking for." He looked at the faces of his two young friends and Benjy. Everyone looked a bit frightened. "Oh, I almost forgot," he added. "We'd better get those." Thad went to the corner of the room and picked up four long pieces of wood. He gave one to each of the girls and one to Benjy.

"Now, don't hit him unless you have to," he said calmly. "If he comes at you, defend yourself. But the main thing is to find out what he's up to."

Thad reached for the door knob and turned it slowly.

Jeanine could feel her heart pounding, and she knew that Bev was excited, too.

Slowly, Thad opened the door. Then the door creaked with a noise that sounded all through the Inn. Thad stood as if he were frozen. Everyone listened. Up above them, someone was moving around in the attic. Thad opened the door still wider. Then with a wave of his arm to the others, he started up the steps.

Later, Bev said that there must have been a hundred steps between the second floor and the attic, but she knew that there were no more than fifteen. One by one they moved up the steps, placing their feet quietly and softly. When Thad had almost reached the top step, he stopped. He put out his hand in the dark and stopped Jeanine and the others. From where he stood, he could see all over the attic. He pulled Jeanine up beside him. Then he moved up another step. Jeanine reached back and pulled Bev up beside her. Benjy was standing just one step below.

They could hear the footsteps of someone very near them. Then the footsteps moved away. In the darkness of the attic they could not see anything. Thad shivered, and he felt cold. Standing beside him, Jeanine felt as if she would never breathe again.

Then a light flashed, and they saw Old Sam at the far side of the attic. He was on his knees by the chimney that came up from the fireplace in the living room. His flashlight played over the bricks, one by one. He reached into his pocket and took out a match. When he struck it, they could tell that he was lighting a lamp. When the light of the lamp flared out over the attic, the youngsters pulled their heads down below the floor of the attic. Slowly they moved back again and watched.

It was Old Sam. There was no mistake about that. He put the lighted lamp on a box near the chimney, and then he moved his hands over the bricks in the chimney.

"Where is Mr. James?" whispered Jeanine.

Thad put his mouth close to Jeanine's ear. "He is probably over there on the steps that come up from the basement. Don't get excited now. Let's watch him for a while."

Old Sam was still feeling the bricks on the chimney. Now and then he seemed to be pulling on a brick. Then he would shake his head and move on to another.

"He's trying to find something in that chimney!" whispered Jeanine in Bev's ear. "Look how he's feeling those bricks!"

Bev felt as if her heart were beating like a drum. Surely Old Sam could hear it! She rested her hand on Jeanine's back. Then it happened. Try as she could, she couldn't stop it. The dust in the old attic was too much for Bev.

"Ah-ah-ah-choo!" A loud sneeze rang through the attic.

Old Sam whirled around. As he turned, his arm hit the lamp on the box, and the lamp fell on the floor. Flames started to lick across the floor as the oil from the lamp spilled on the dry boards. Old Sam grabbed an old piece of cloth and started beating at the fire.

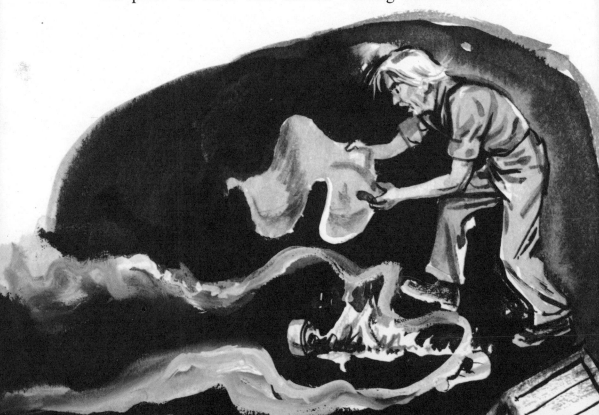

"Stay where you are, Sam!" cried Mr. James' voice
from the other side of the attic.

Thad, Jeanine, Bev, and Benjy moved quickly up the
steps and stood on the floor of the attic.

For a moment, Old Sam didn't move. Then he
started running. When he saw the youngsters and Benjy,
he turned and ran the other way. But Mr. James was
standing there at the head of the steps.

"You'd better give up, Sam!" shouted Benjy.

Old Sam looked like a trapped animal. He stood
there in the middle of the attic looking all around him.
His eyes darted from corner to corner. Then he started
running toward a window.

"You'll never get me!" he shouted. There was a loud
crash as he jumped through the window of the attic.

No one moved. They all waited to hear the sound of the body as it fell through the air to the ground below. But the sound never came!

"He's on the roof! Get outside as fast as you can," cried Mr. James.

Everyone rushed down the steps. When Mrs. James saw the youngsters rush through the living room, she ran after them. Through the kitchen they ran and down the steps into the garden.

Thad, Jeanine, and Bev would never forget what they saw next. Standing in the moonlight, Mr. James was looking up at the roof of the Inn. There, at least forty feet above the ground, was the small body of Old Sam clinging to the edge of the roof.

"Get a ladder someone," cried Bev. "He's going to fall."

"You'll never reach him with a ladder," said Mr. James. "There isn't a ladder in this town that will reach that roof. I don't know what we can do."

"Maybe I can reach him from that tree," said Thad. He pointed to a tall tree that hung over the edge of the roof above the place where Old Sam was.

"You'll not do anything like that, Thad," said Mrs. James firmly. "You'll get hurt. There must be some other way to reach him."

Everyone was talking at once, looking at the still, small figure at the edge of the roof.

"I feel so helpless," cried Jeanine. "Can't someone help him down from there? He's going to fall!"

Then Old Sam started to move. As slowly as a snail, he was moving back up the steep roof toward the window. As everyone watched, a head came out of the window, and they could hear a voice.

"That's right, Sam, just take it easy," the voice said. "Take it easy now. Keep coming. That's a good man. Hold out your hand now."

"That's Benjy," cried Bev. "Benjy is up there in that window helping Old Sam."

It was Benjy who was leaning out of the window holding out his hand to Old Sam. As they watched hardly daring to breathe, Benjy's hand reached Old Sam, and they saw the old man crawl back into the attic through the window.

"Into the house, everyone," cried Mr. James. "Don't let him get away again."

But they didn't have to worry about Old Sam. When they came into the living room, a very sad looking old man was sitting in the big chair with his head down. Beside him stood Benjy. He was patting the old man on the back. Benjy's face looked old and tired. He looked up as Mr. and Mrs. James and the youngsters came in.

Pearls for Everyone

Old Sam didn't move. He did not hold his head up.
Thad thought he had never seen a sadder figure anywhere.

"The poor man is shivering," said Mrs. James. "I'll
get some coffee." She turned and went into the kitchen.

Benjy lighted a fire in the fireplace. The warmth of
the fire flooded the big, friendly room. Still Old Sam
didn't move. Only when Mrs. James came in with a cup
of coffee and put it into his hands did he look up. There
were tears in his eyes.

"I'm not shivering because I'm cold, Mrs. James," said
Old Sam. "I'm scared half to death." He took a sip of
coffee and leaned back in the chair. He looked at the face
of each person in the room.

"I want to tell you everything," he mumbled through his chattering teeth. "Everything right from the beginning!"

"Now, drink your coffee first," said Mr. James kindly. "We can wait for your story, Sam. We're not going to do anything to hurt you."

Old Sam sipped his coffee slowly. Jeanine thought he would never finish it. Sitting on the floor, she slowly moved over so that she could see his face clearly. It wasn't a mean face at all. It was just the face of a very tired, very old man.

Everyone sat quietly waiting for Sam to finish his coffee. When he put his cup down, he tried to smile.

"I wouldn't have hurt anyone, you know," Old Sam said. "You must believe that. It wouldn't have been worth it to hurt anyone. I didn't even want to scare you."

"But I thought I could find it last night, and I....well, I guess I scared you." He looked at Thad, Jeanine, and Bev. He smiled at Mrs. James. "For that, I'm sorry, real sorry. It was a foolish thing to do."

"What were you looking for? What's in the chimney?" cried Bev. Her face was glowing with excitement.

Old Sam held up his hand. "Wait, please," he answered. "I'll get to that. Let me start from the beginning."

"It started a long time ago," Old Sam said slowly. "In fact, it started over fifty years ago. I had a partner, Ed Clark, who fished with me. We worked as fishermen in many parts of the world. Ed was a restless one, never wanting to stay anywhere very long. But he was a good man, an honest man. You have to know that." He paused, and his eyes seemed to be looking far, far away.

"We were young when we first came to this Inn. We stayed up there in that attic because there was no bed here below for us. Whenever Ed and I would come to Longcliff, we'd stay in the Inn. You see, Ed Clark lived in this Inn at one time. He spent most of his years as a child in this Inn. That's how he knew about the well, and the tunnel, and the steps in that wall. He never told me about them until...." The old man sat there as if he were dreaming.

"Ed was a wise man. He saved his money, and he saved it well. He bought pearls, lots of pearls, because he believed that pearls would always be worth something. Pearls were pretty cheap then, and Ed had a lot of them. It was something we didn't talk about. I knew he had them, but I never knew where he kept them.

"Well, Ed and I went all over the world. Sometimes we were so poor that we didn't know where our next meal was coming from. One time, when we were really hungry, I asked Ed why he didn't sell one of his pearls. He said he was keeping those for his old age, and that was the end of that. We stayed hungry until we got another job."

"The pearls! That's what you've been looking for!" cried Jeanine. "Are they in the Inn? Are they?"

Old Sam smiled. "You kids are really excited, aren't you?" he said. "Yes, I was looking for the pearls. But wait and let me tell you more. You see, Ed died a couple of years ago, and for the first time in many years I was all alone. Ed left me a letter, and when I opened it, I had the surprise of my life."

"He told you where the pearls were!" said Bev. "And he had made a map for you!"

Old Sam patted Bev's head. "You know," he said with a twinkle, "if I had a daughter, I'd want her to be just as smart as you are! Yes, he left me a map and a letter telling me that the pearls were here in Longcliff Inn. For a while, I thought Ed must have been crazy. But the more I thought about it, the more I believed him. I remembered that there were a couple of times when we were staying here in the Inn and Ed disappeared for a while. The more I thought about it, the more I knew that Ed had really hidden the pearls in this Inn. Well, you must know the rest. I came here to Longcliff and moved into the cabin. Then I started looking around the Inn here."

Old Sam grinned at Benjy. "You didn't help me a bit, you know. I tried to ask you questions, but you wouldn't tell me anything. I didn't know where the well was, and it took me some time to find it. After all, I had to work at night. When I finally found the well and the tunnel, I knew that Ed's map must be right."

Thad jumped to his feet. "Then the pearls must still be here!" he cried. "Let's find them!"

"I've looked for them, boy," said Old Sam. "Oh, how I've looked for them. I've been all over this old Inn, and they aren't where Ed said they were."

"Just where did Ed say that he had put them?" asked Mr. James. "Maybe I can help you. After all, I've lived here almost fifty years."

"I know you have, Mr. James," said Old Sam. "You don't remember me. But you were here when Ed and I used to come here. You were a young man then, and you were very busy keeping everyone happy and well fed."

"Sam, could I see that map?" asked Mr. James. He was almost as excited as the youngsters were.

"It's right here," answered Sam. Slowly he pulled a piece of paper out of his pocket. He got up and spread the paper on a table near the light. Everyone crowded around and looked at it.

Mr. James studied the map for a long time, turning it this way and that. Then he smiled. "It's a good map," he said, "but your friend Ed was a little mixed up. Now, you were working tonight at the chimney on this end of the attic." He pointed to a spot on the map. "That chimney wasn't in this old Inn when you and Ed were coming here. You see, we've had to change a few things in the old Inn through the years. Ed's chimney must have been the old one, and it's at the other end of the attic, behind a wall. We don't use that chimney anymore."

"Let's go!" shouted Thad, and he started to run out of the room. Everyone followed him as he leaped up the steps to the second floor, through the door and up the steps into the attic. Mr. James had brought a lantern with him, and in the soft shadows of the attic everyone gathered near the wall where the old chimney was supposed to be.

"Right here, Benjy," said Mr. James. Benjy stepped up, and he had an iron bar in his hands. He struck the wall and opened a hole in it. Bev, Jeanine, and Thad helped Benjy as he tore the thin wall down. Then they all gasped. There was the chimney!

"Now," said Mr. James, "I think we should let Sam take over at this point. Sam, you know where to look. Why don't you try your luck?"

Sam moved as if he were in a dream. For a long time he stood looking at the chimney. His eyes moved over each brick. Then he finally put out his hand and touched one of the bricks.

"This should be the one," he said softly. Gently he moved the brick until it came out. Then he stepped back.

"You do it!" he said to Jeanine. "Put your hand in that hole and see what you find."

Jeanine stood on tiptoes and started to put her hand in the hole. Then she stopped and looked at the others.

"Well, go on, Jeanine," cried Bev. "What are you waiting for? I can hardly stand this!"

Jeanine put her hand into the hole in the chimney. When she pulled it out, she held a small sack in it.

"Open it! Open it, Jeanine!" cried Thad. His hands were fumbling with the sack, and so were Bev's.

"Oh dear! I don't think I can stand this either!" sighed Mrs. James.

The youngsters were still fumbling with the sack. Mr. James laughed, and the sound echoed through the big attic. "Here," Mr. James said, "let me have it. I think one pair of hands can do the job. Sam, you open the sack. After all it's yours."

In the light of the lantern, Sam slowly opened the sack. He reached his hand in, and when the light struck the pearls, everyone cheered!

Suddenly Old Sam felt very weak. He sat down in the middle of the floor, and the pearls spilled on the floor beside him. When he looked up, the tears were streaming down his face.

"They're yours, Sam," said Mr. James softly. "Take them and use them well."

"You're kind to me," said Sam through his tears. "I've scared you half to death, I've broken into your house, and still you're kind to me."

Into the hands of each person in that attic, Old Sam placed a pearl. "They're yours," he said. "I don't need all of them. Please keep them, won't you? I'm sure Ed would have wanted me to do this." (1724)

Glossary

PRONUNCIATION SYMBOLS

By permission. From Webster's Seventh New Collegiate Dictionary, copyright 1967 by G. & C. Merriam Company, publishers of the Merriam-Webster Dictionaries.

a as in map	i as in tip	s as in less
ā as in day	ī as in side	sh as in shy
ä as in cot	j as in job	t as in tie
á as in father	k as in kin	th as in thin
aù as in out	l as in pool	th as in then
b as in baby	m as in dim	ü as in rule
ch as in chin	n as in no	ù as in pull
d as in did	ŋ as in sing	v as in give
e as in bed	ō as in bone	w as in we
ē as in easy	ȯ as in saw	y as in yard
f as in cuff	ȯi as in coin	z as in zone
g as in go	p as in lip	zh as in vision
h as in hat	r as in rarity	ə as in banana, collect

bustling /'bəs-(ə)liŋ/ moving briskly, busily. 7

emphatically /im-'fat-ik(ə-)lē/ speaking with emphasis and force. 39

flicker /'flik-ər/ to waver unsteadily. 8

glint /'glint/ to shine with tiny bright flashes. 6

gurgling /'gər-g(ə-)liŋŋ/ flowing in broken, irregular current. 46

hesitate /'hez-ə-tāt/ to hold back, to pause. 65

intently /in-'tent-lē/ fixing the mind on something. 31

murmur /'mər-mər/ soft or gentle speaking. 9

panel /'pan-əl/ a flat piece of wood forming part of a surface. 19

plunge /'pləng/ to enter suddenly. 8

shiver /'shiv-ər/ to tremble or quiver. 20

shrug /'shrəg/ to raise the shoulders showing indifference. 43

snoop /'snüp/ to look or pry in a sneaky manner. 39

stern /'stərn/ expressing severe displeasure. 42

swoop/'swüp/ to move with a sweep. 25

twitter /'twit-ər/ the chirping of birds. 16

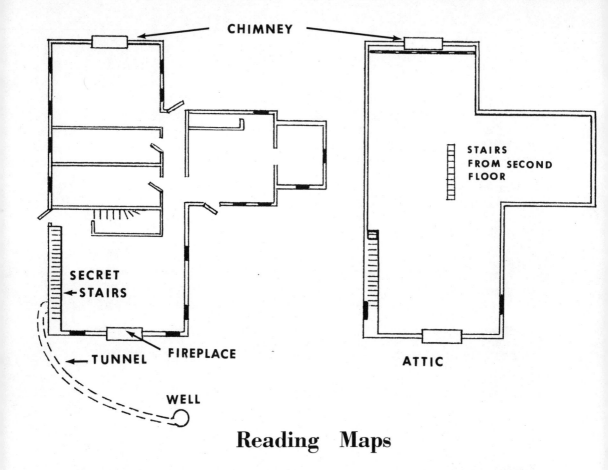

CHIMNEY

STAIRS FROM SECOND FLOOR

SECRET STAIRS

TUNNEL FIREPLACE

WELL

ATTIC

Reading Maps

"That scream sure scared me last night," said Jeanine as she and Bev were eating breakfast. "What do you think it could have been?"

"I'm sure it wasn't a raccoon," said Bev. "And I think we'd better forget about it."

"Forget about it?" cried Thad as he entered the kitchen. "Are you out of your minds? Someone or something is not playing a joke. I want to find out what this is all about."

"All right," said Jeanine. "Let's start looking for clues. How could someone get into the attic without our knowing it?"

"I haven't the slightest idea," said Bev.

"I think I do," said Thad.

What gave Thad the clue that led to the solving of the mystery?

Longcliff Inn

People who travel have always needed places in which to sleep and eat. Early in American history, the business of providing hotels and inns developed. Inns such as the one at Longcliff accommodated travelers, traders, sailors, and adventurers. Some inns provided only lodging, but others such as the one at Longcliff provided both food and lodging. The first American inns were located along the Atlantic. Thus, Longcliff Inn was a convenient stopping place for Ed Clark and his fishing buddy, Sam.

Stories are often based on facts. Read the first paragraph below. What facts do you find in it? Read the rest of the material. What facts do you find? How has the author presented the facts in an interesting way? Give examples.

Longcliff Inn was built over one hundred years ago. It overlooked the harbor, and seafaring travelers found it a convenient place in which to stay for a night or two or even longer. Then it was a happy place filled with boisterous sailor voices. Now, one hundred years later, Longcliff Inn was a quiet place and few lodgers stayed there. The innkeepers, Mr. and Mrs. James, now had time to entertain their young guests who were so fond of the old inn.

Longcliff Inn was a large inn surrounded by tall trees. The trees cut off much of the light, making the inn look dark and mysterious. The three floors of the inn contained many rooms which could accommodate lodgers. Thad, Jeanine, and Bev had visited the Inn many times, but they had never seen all of the rooms in it.

But the rooms were not all that Thad, Jeanine, and Bev had not seen. What would you have done if you had discovered the hidden stairs and the tunnel?

Mystery Words

There are ten scrambled mystery words in the box on this page. A scrambled mystery word belongs in each one of the ten sentences under the box. Make ten lines on a piece of paper and number the lines from 1 to 10. Then read the first sentence below. Look at the mystery words and find the word that belongs in the first sentence. Write the word, correctly spelled, on the first line on your paper. Read each of the other sentences, find its correct scrambled mystery word, and write it on your paper.

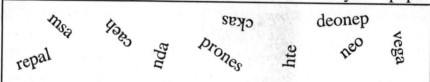

1. Old XXX looked like a trapped animal.
2. A door XXXXXX and light streamed up the steps.
3. Then XXX door of the cabin opened, and someone was coming out.
4. His hands were fumbling with the XXXX, and so were Bev's.
5. From their windows one could look out at the harbor XXX the ocean beyond.
6. He XXXX the board a push, and it moved.
7. His eyes moved over XXXX brick.
8. They continued to look at the well, each XXXXXX wondering.
9. The night before had been a frightening XXX, and they had not slept well.
10. Even when they were hungry, Ed would not sell a XXXXX.